Danielle
the Daisy
Fairy

For Danielle Dawkins,
who has lots of magic of her own!

Special thanks to Narinder Dhami

No part of this work may be reproduced, stored in a retrieval system,
or transmitted in any form or by any means, electronic, mechanical,
photocopying, recording, or otherwise, without written permission
of the publisher. For information regarding permission, write to
Rainbow Magic Limited c/o HIT Entertainment,
830 South Greenville Avenue, Allen, TX 75002-3320.

ISBN-10: 0-545-07095-3
ISBN-13: 978-0-545-07095-9

12 11 10 9 8 7 6 5 4 3 2   10 11 12 13/0

Printed in the U.S.A.

First Scholastic Printing, February 2009

Danielle
the Daisy
Fairy

by Daisy Meadows

SCHOLASTIC INC.

New York   Toronto   London   Auckland   Sydney
Mexico City   New Delhi   Hong Kong   Buenos Aires

I need the magic petals' powers,
To give my castle garden flowers.
I plan to use my magic well
To work against the fairies' spell.

From my wand ice magic flies,
Frosty bolts through fairy skies.
This is the crafty spell I weave
To bring the petals back to me.

Contents

A Mysterious Message

"Oh!" Rachel Walker panted as she hiked up the steep hill. "I'm really out of breath."

"Me, too," Kirsty Tate, Rachel's best friend, agreed. "Even Buttons looks a little tired, and you know how he always bounces around."

Buttons, the Walkers's shaggy dog, was

trotting along next to Rachel with his pink tongue hanging out.

"It'll be worth it when we get to the top, girls," called Rachel's dad. He was walking behind them with Mrs. Walker and Kirsty's parents. "The view will be fantastic. And so will the food," he said patting a large straw picnic basket.

A few moments later, Rachel and Kirsty reached the top of the hill.

Both girls gasped as they
gazed around.
"You were right, Dad!"
Rachel smiled.
"It was worth it,"
Kirsty added.
The sun was
shining, and
the countryside
that spread out
below them
looked beautiful.
Lush green fields
stretched in every
direction. Nestled
in a little valley,
the girls could see the
thatched-roof cottages
of Blossom Village.

"Blossom Village almost looks Fairyland-size from here!" Rachel whispered to Kirsty.

Kirsty laughed. She and Rachel knew more about fairies than anyone else! The fairies were their special friends, and the girls had visited Fairyland many times.

"Look, there's Blossom Hall," said Mr. Tate, pointing at a bigger building beyond the village. The Tates and the Walkers were spending their spring vacation in the old mansion that was now a country hotel. "Even that looks small from up here!"

Kirsty and Rachel shared a smile as they gazed at Blossom Hall. Their stay at the old hotel had led to a whole new fairy adventure. On their first day at the hall, they had met Tia the Tulip Fairy in the beautiful gardens. Tia had whisked them off to Fairyland, where King Oberon and Queen Titania had explained that Jack Frost and his goblins had tried to steal the Petal Fairies' seven magic petals. The petals were very important. Their magic made sure that all flowers were healthy and beautiful! In a battle of spells between the fairies and Jack Frost, the petals had whirled away and become lost in the human world. Jack Frost had sent his goblins to get them back. Now Rachel and Kirsty were trying to help the fairies find the magic petals before the goblins did.

"Where should we have our picnic?" asked Mrs. Tate. She glanced up at the sky, where dark clouds were threatening to cover the sun. "Oh, I hope it isn't going to rain. The weather forecast said it might."

"Well, I brought a big umbrella, just in case," Mr. Walker

replied, "but let's hope it holds off until we get back to Blossom Hall."

"Look, there's a nice spot over there by the stream," Kirsty said, pointing to the other side of the hill. "That might be a good place for our picnic."

"Good idea," Mr. Walker agreed.

The stream was narrow but long. The girls could see that the crystal-clear water bubbled and flowed over rocks and pebbles, running all the way down to the other side of the hill.

"Look, Rachel," Kirsty said in a low voice as their parents unpacked the picnic basket. "The daisies all around us are wilting!"

"I know," Rachel whispered back. "I noticed when we were walking up the hill. I hope we find Danielle the Daisy Fairy's magic petal today!"

"Yes, we've found five petals already, but we need all seven," Kirsty added.

Rachel nodded seriously. Both girls knew that they had to return all the petals to Fairyland. It was the only way the petal magic would work and keep flowers everywhere blooming brightly.

"This is a perfect spot," said Mrs. Walker, as she poured water into Buttons' bowl. "I hope you all worked up an appetite on that long walk."

Rachel and Kirsty nodded enthusiastically as Mr. Tate opened the picnic basket and began handing out wrapped sandwiches and bags of chips. As they ate, Buttons munched on some dog treats.

"We have blueberry muffins for dessert," Mrs. Tate said with a smile, pulling a large plastic container out of the basket.

"Yum!" said Rachel happily.

"That's just what I was going to say!" Her dad laughed.

Kirsty and Rachel ate their sandwiches, enjoying the view. As Kirsty was finishing off her chips, she gazed at the little stream bubbling its way down the hill toward a patch of trees. *I wonder where it ends up?* she thought.

Suddenly, to Kirsty's amazement, she saw a beautiful cloud of silver fairy dust rising from the trees.

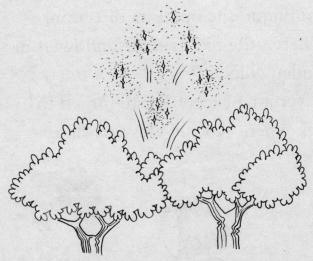

Kirsty almost choked on the last bite of her sandwich! As she watched, the silvery sparkles began to drift through the air toward her.

Kirsty knew she and Rachel had to make sure their parents didn't spot the fairy dust. Quickly, she nudged Rachel,

who was sitting next to her. Rachel
glanced up, and her eyes widened.

"Look, everyone!" Rachel said quickly,
pointing in the opposite direction.
"There's the big field of sunflowers in
Leafley village."

Everyone except Kirsty turned to
look where Rachel was pointing.

Meanwhile, Kirsty watched as the silvery sparkles began to form themselves into words. They seemed to float right in front of her:

Look around, there's more to see.
A fairy friend says: follow me!

Then the cloud of sparkles streamed away and disappeared on the breeze.

Still tingling with excitement, Kirsty
turned to her mother. "Mom, is it OK if
Rachel and I go
exploring before we
eat our muffins?"
she asked eagerly.
Mrs. Tate nodded.
"Don't go far,
though," added
Mr. Walker, "and be back
in half an hour."

Rachel and Kirsty scrambled to their
feet and hurried off, following the stream
toward the woods.

"The sparkles spelled out a message,
Rachel!" Kirsty told her friend,
her eyes shining. She repeated the
little poem.

"One of the Petal Fairies must have

sent it," Rachel guessed, her face bright with excitement.

The girls soon reached the trees. As they stood on the edge of the little forest, wondering where to go next, they heard a soft whooshing sound. Suddenly, tiny silver sparkles began shooting out from behind an oak tree.

The girls hurried over.

"Hi, girls!" Danielle the Daisy Fairy called, peeking out from behind the tree trunk and grinning at them. "I've been waiting for you!"

Daisy, Daisy

Danielle danced out from behind the tree as Kirsty and Rachel glanced at each other, grinning. The little fairy looked very daisylike in a bright yellow top and a white skirt with pink trim. Her wings were pink-tipped, too, and a daisy-shaped barrette held back her long blond hair.

"It's great to see you, girls," Danielle said. "I really need your help. One of Jack Frost's goblins has found my magic daisy petal, and until I get it back, daisies and all the white flowers in the world will be in trouble!"

"Oh!" Rachel gasped. "Is the goblin in these woods?" Danielle nodded. "Follow me," she said. "But remember, girls, the goblins have a wand with Jack Frost's icy magic to help them. So we have to be careful!" Danielle flew off, and Kirsty and Rachel followed the tiny, sparkling fairy

deeper into the woods.
After a few moments
Danielle stopped behind
a large oak tree with a
thick gnarled trunk. She
motioned to the girls,
putting a finger to her lips.

Kirsty and Rachel peeked around
the tree trunk. In front of them was a large
clearing, and the green grass was spotted
with wilting daisies. A goblin sat on a rock
in the middle of the clearing,
making a daisy chain. He
had collected a bunch
of the flowers, ready to
add to the chain. The
daisies were in a pile
next to him.

"Look at those daisies the goblin has collected," Danielle whispered.

Rachel and Kirsty stared at the pile of daisies and immediately noticed that

they looked fresh and healthy. Their centers were a bright and sunny yellow. The girls knew that meant the magic petal must be very close by!

The goblin's chain was growing quickly, and he was singing a silly made-up song as he threaded the daisies together.

"*Daisy, daisy, I'm not lazy,*" he sang loudly, twirling a daisy in his knobby

green hand. *"Daisy, daisy, I'm not crazy! I just love my daisies!"*

Kirsty clapped her hands over her ears. "He's all out of tune!" she complained.

"The other goblins can't be far away," Rachel said in a low voice. "Jack Frost told them to stick together this time, remember?"

"This one doesn't have the wand, either," Danielle pointed out. "Let's try to get my petal back before the others show up."

But before they could do anything, they heard noises from the other side of the woods.

A minute later, a large group of
noisy goblins burst into the
clearing. Rachel, Kirsty,
and Danielle
glanced at one
another in dismay.
Danielle let out
a little groan
when she saw
the icy wand
in the hands of
the smallest goblin.

"What are you
doing?" demanded a
big goblin, going
over to the one with
the daisies.

"Making a daisy chain,"
the goblin replied.

"Lazybones!" snapped the smallest goblin. "We've been searching all over the hill for the magic petal, and you've been sitting here taking a nice rest!"

"It's not fair!" the big goblin grumbled. "I'm telling Jack Frost!" Looking annoyed, the seated goblin threw down his daisy chain and jumped off the rock. "All right!" he snapped.

"I'll help you look now." He tromped off, pouting as he poked around the daisy patches.

Rachel, Kirsty, and Danielle watched as all the others followed, except for the big goblin. With a nasty grin on his face, he picked up the long daisy chain and draped it around his shoulders like a feather boa.

"Hey!" the goblin who had made the chain yelled, racing over to the big goblin. "Give that back!" he screeched. "It's mine!"

"No, I won't!" the big goblin refused. "I look nice!"

Furious, the first goblin grabbed one
end of the chain of daisies. But before
he could pull it away, the big goblin
grabbed the other end, and the
delicate chain broke immediately and
fell apart.

"Now look at what you've done!"
yelled the first goblin. They both threw
the broken ends down on the ground.

"It was your fault!" the
big goblin grumbled.
He drew back his
big, knobby foot
and kicked the
pile of daisies into
the air. They all
were flying.

"You go and
search these woods

for the magic petal!" he roared at the others when he saw them watching. "We have to find it before those pesky fairies do!"

All the goblins stomped off across the clearing, searching for the petal. The big goblin came straight toward the tree where Danielle and the girls were hiding!

As the goblin came closer, Rachel noticed something magical. Everywhere

the goblin stepped, the daisies around his feet burst into bright blossoms! But as soon as he moved away from them, they died again.

Rachel knew this could only mean one thing.

"Look at the goblin's foot when he lifts it up," she whispered to Kirsty and Danielle. "I think the magic petal is stuck underneath!"

Step By Step

Danielle and the girls watched closely as the goblin lifted his foot to take another step. Sure enough, the sparkling magic petal was stuck to the bottom of his big green heel.

"How are we going to get it away from him?" asked Rachel.

Kirsty thought hard. "I have an

idea. . . ." she said slowly. "Danielle, could you turn us into fairies, please?"

"Of course!" Danielle replied.

She flew above Rachel and Kirsty and, with a flick of her fairy wand, showered them with glittering magical sparkles. The girls felt the familiar rush of excitement as they began to shrink. Within seconds they were the same size as Danielle, with shining fairy wings on their backs.

"Let's go!" Kirsty cried, flying off into the clearing. Rachel and Danielle followed.

The other goblins had disappeared into the woods now, so only the big goblin was still searching the clearing. He seemed annoyed as he looked halfheartedly for the magic petal. Kirsty wondered what he'd do if he knew it was stuck to his very own foot!

"Hello!" she called, hovering above him with Rachel and Danielle beside her.

The goblin glanced up. "Pesky fairies!" he muttered grumpily. "You're always turning up out of nowhere."

"You've been working very hard, haven't you?" Kirsty said kindly.

The goblin frowned. "Yes, I have!" he snapped.

"So you must be tired," Kirsty went on. "After all, that other goblin had a nice rest, but you didn't."

"It wasn't fair!" the big goblin moaned. Rachel and Danielle grinned at each other as they realized what Kirsty had planned! "Well, now it's your turn to take a rest," Rachel chimed in. "Why don't you lie down?" She pointed at the rock where the first goblin had been sitting.

The goblin yawned. "Maybe I will."

As the goblin walked back to the rock, the daisies at his feet bloomed and wilted with his every step. Danielle, Kirsty, and

Rachel glanced nervously at one another, but luckily the goblin didn't notice. He sat down on the rock and yawned again.

Winking at the girls, Danielle lifted her wand, and a shower of sparkles floated down onto the broken daisy chain. The daisies immediately bunched up into a soft, snuggly white pillow.

The goblin looked at the comfy pillow. "Nobody will notice if I take a quick nap," he said to himself, glancing around the clearing to make sure the other goblins were nowhere in sight. "After all, I *have* worked the hardest today. . . ."

He put his head on the daisy pillow,
lifted his feet onto the rock, and closed his
eyes. Now Danielle, Kirsty, and Rachel
could see the magic petal sparkling on
the bottom of the goblin's foot.

They waited, afraid to move, until they
heard heavy, rumbling snores echo
through the clearing.

"The goblin's asleep," Kirsty whispered. "Now we can peel the petal off his foot. Come on!"

Quickly, the three fairies flew down to the snoring goblin. They were just peeling the petal away from his toes when they heard a noise behind them. A second later, the other goblins came crashing through the trees and into the clearing. The three friends gasped in surprise.

"Hey!" the smallest goblin shouted angrily, pointing at the goblin on the rock. "He's taking a nap while we're doing all the work!"

"Look!" yelled another. "Fairies! I bet they're looking for the magic petal, too. Let's get them!"

And all the goblins rushed across the clearing, straight toward Danielle, Kirsty, and Rachel.

Danielle in Trouble

Just then, the goblin on the rock woke up and spotted Danielle and the girls.

"Help!" he yelled, kicking at them. "I'm being attacked by fairies!"

Danielle, Rachel, and Kirsty had no choice but to leave the petal behind. They quickly flew straight up into the air to escape from the gang of goblins that was charging toward them.

"What do we do now?" asked Kirsty, as they hovered above the rock. Looking down, they could still see the petal, which was now hanging off the goblin's foot.

"I'll get rid of these pesky fairies!" the smallest goblin boasted eagerly, lifting Jack Frost's wand.

"*I don't want a doggie, a pig, or a whale,*" he shouted. "*But send to that rock big pieces of hail!*" The smallest goblin pointed the wand at the rock.

"Don't point that thing at me!" the big goblin shouted in alarm. He jumped up and ran for cover. As he did, the magic petal fell off his foot and landed on the rock.

Danielle immediately swooped down to grab it, followed closely by Kirsty and Rachel. But big, icy pieces of hail suddenly began to rain down onto the rock from the sky.

Kirsty gasped in horror when she saw how huge the hailstones were. *It's like playing dodgeball with humongous frozen kickballs!* she thought. She and her friends zipped back and forth to avoid being hit.

Just as Danielle reached out for the daisy petal, a hailstone struck her shoulder and sent her spinning toward the ground. Rachel and Kirsty immediately flew to help her, managing to catch her in midair.

They each took one of the fairy's arms and helped her fly safely to the edge of the clearing, away from the hailstorm. "Are you OK, Danielle?" Kirsty asked. Danielle looked very shaken, and Rachel bit her lip as she waited for the fairy's reply. "I'm OK, but I lost my wand!" Danielle exclaimed, rubbing her shoulder.

"I must have dropped it when I
got hit."

"Look, there it is!" Rachel said,
pointing back at the rock. Through the
shower of hailstones, they could see
the wand lying next to the magic petal.

Danielle, Kirsty, and Rachel looked at
one another, wondering what to do next.

Just then, there was a shout from one of the goblins.

"There's the magic petal!" he cried, pointing at the rock.

"And that's a fairy wand next to it!" added another goblin in delight.

The goblins gathered around the rock, staring at the petal and Danielle's wand.

No one dared to get too close, because the hailstones were still raining down with full force.

"The fairies can't get the magic petal now, but neither can we!" the big goblin said, scowling at the goblin with the wand. "What a silly spell!"

"Danielle, maybe if Rachel and I were human again, we could dodge the hailstones and grab the petal," Kirsty suggested.

Danielle's wings drooped. "But I can't turn you back to normal without my wand," she said. She looked as if she were about to cry.

"Maybe I can help!" said a kind voice behind them.

Danielle, Kirsty, and Rachel spun around. To their amazement, a girl was standing among the trees, smiling at them!

A Helping Hand

Kirsty and Rachel were so surprised, neither of them could say a word. The fairies were supposed to be a secret! The two girls were the only humans who knew about them. What was going to happen now?

"Don't worry," the girl said quickly. "I won't tell anyone. I've always wanted to see a fairy, but I never, ever thought I would!"

Danielle smiled and turned to Rachel and Kirsty. "It's OK," she said. "She's going to be our friend!" And she fluttered over to the girl. "I'm Danielle, this is Rachel, and this is Kirsty."

"My name's Rebecca Wilson," the girl replied, watching with delight as Danielle, Rachel, and Kirsty hovered in front of her.

"Well, Rebecca, we really need your help!" Danielle explained. "But you must promise never to tell anyone that you've met the fairies."

"I promise," Rebecca said seriously.

Quickly, Danielle explained about Jack Frost and his goblins stealing the magic petals.

Rebecca looked horrified. "Jack Frost must be very mean!" she said. "What can I do to help?"

"Oh!" Kirsty gasped, as she suddenly thought of something. "Rachel, why didn't we bring one of our umbrellas with us?"

"Oh, that's too bad. We could have given it to Rebecca, and she could have run through the hailstones and grabbed the petal for us," Rachel agreed.

Rebecca looked confused. "I have an umbrella in my backpack," she said, reaching into her bag and taking out a pink umbrella. "But I don't see any hailstones!"

Danielle laughed. "Come and look!" Danielle and the girls led Rebecca to the edge of the clearing, where the goblins were still standing around the rock.

"I'll get the magic petal!" one of them was boasting. He reached out for it, but quickly jumped back as hailstone hit his hand. "Ouch!"

"Leave this to me," said another goblin importantly. He made a grab for the petal and then he, too, pulled his hand back. "Ow, that hurt!"

"Jack Frost wants that petal!" the big goblin declared. "And if we bring him the fairy wand, too, he'll be so impressed!"

"Now I see why you need the umbrella!" whispered Rebecca. "I'll hold it for you."

"Thank you!" Danielle, Rachel, and Kirsty chorused.

Rebecca walked bravely out into the clearing with Danielle and the girls flying beside her.

"Um — *Hail, hail, please go away nice and quick,*" the smallest goblin chanted. He was desperately trying to think of a spell to stop the hail.

"That's horrible!" the others complained. Suddenly, the goblins noticed Rebecca and the girls. Rebecca quickly opened her umbrella and pointed it straight at the goblins. They shrieked with fright and started to back away. Rebecca hurried forward. When she held the umbrella over the rock, the hailstones bounced right off it.

"They're going to get the magic petal *and* the fairy wand!" shouted the big goblin. He frowned as Danielle, Rachel, and Kirsty darted under the cover of the umbrella. "We need that spell!" the goblin growled.

"*We don't like this nasty hail!*" the smallest goblin yelled. "*I wish we could all go home!*"

"That doesn't even rhyme!" another goblin yelled furiously.

Meanwhile, Danielle had grabbed her wand, and Kirsty and Rachel had picked up the magic petal together.

"*Hail, hail, go away,*" shouted the smallest goblin,

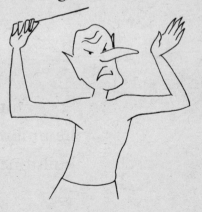

waving the wand, *"And don't come back until May!"*

Immediately, the hailstones stopped. Danielle, Rachel, Kirsty, and Rebecca exchanged panicked looks as all the goblins hurried forward to block their escape.

"Leave my friends alone!" Rebecca said bravely, waving her umbrella.

"Oh no you don't," insisted the smallest goblin as the others stuck out their tongues. "We're taking that petal to Jack Frost!"

Daisy Delight

Rachel thought fast. She turned to Danielle and whispered something in her ear.

Danielle's worried face broke into a big smile. She waved her wand back and forth, and a shower of fairy dust fell onto the daisy pillow, which was still lying on the ground. Quickly, the magic sparkles changed the pillow back into the chain of daisies.

As Danielle, the girls, and Rebecca watched, the daisy chain flew into the air and began to wind itself tightly around the goblins.

"Help!" shrieked the smallest goblin. "What's happening?" He raised his wand to try to cast another spell, but he couldn't lift his arm. The daisy chain was wrapped too tightly around it!

"Let us go!" yelled the biggest goblin as the daisy chain tied itself into a neat little bow.

"It's a bouquet of goblins!" said Rachel with a grin, watching as the goblins struggled helplessly.

"My petal magic has made the daisy chain extra-strong!" laughed Danielle. Then she, Kirsty, Rachel, and Rebecca hurried out of the clearing. Behind them, they could hear the goblins fighting and

arguing as they tried to break out of the daisy chain.

"It will take the goblins a while to get free," Danielle went on. "And, by then, I'll have taken my beautiful petal back to Fairyland!"

With a wave of Danielle's wand, the daisy petal shrank down to its Fairyland size. Then it floated out of Kirsty's and Rachel's hands and over to Danielle. Another sprinkling of fairy magic made Rachel and Kirsty their normal size again, too. Rebecca looked very surprised. "I didn't know you were girls, too!" she exclaimed.

The girls nodded.

"Rachel and Kirsty are best friends with the fairies," Danielle explained. "And now you're one of our friends as well!"

"I'm glad I was able to help!" Rebecca said as Rachel and Kirsty grinned at her. "Now I'd better get back, or my family will wonder where I am. We're having a picnic on the other side of the woods."

"Thank you for your help, and good-bye!" Danielle called, waving.

"Yes, thank you, Rebecca!" said Rachel and Kirsty together.

"Good-bye!" Rebecca called, as she made her way through the trees. "I'll never, ever forget the day I met a real fairy!"

"We'd better go too, Rachel," Kirsty said after Rebecca was out of sight.

Danielle nodded. "Thank you so much for all your help, girls," she told them. "Now, you only have one more magic petal to find. Good luck!" And, holding her daisy petal tightly, Danielle disappeared in a shower of fairy dust.

"Wasn't Rebecca nice?" remarked Rachel, as she and Kirsty hurried back to their parents.

Kirsty nodded. "I don't know what we would have done if she hadn't shown up!" she replied.

When they stepped out of the woods,

Buttons rushed to meet them, his tail wagging.

Their parents were napping on the picnic blanket, but Mrs. Tate sat up as the girls ran over.

"We saved you some muffins," she said kindly, motioning to the picnic basket. "Did you have a nice walk?"

The girls nodded, laughing at Buttons who was now rolling around on his back in a patch of springy white daisies.

"Well, I certainly didn't notice all those beautiful daisies when we were on our way up the hill!" Mrs. Tate said, looking around her. The grass was now starred with the little white flowers. "Aren't they pretty?"

Rachel and Kirsty nodded and shared a secret smile. All the daisies were blooming beautifully now that Danielle's magic petal was back in Fairyland — where it belonged!

THE PETAL FAIRIES

Now Danielle the Daisy Fairy has her
magic petal back. Next, Rachel
and Kirsty must help

Ella

the Rose Fairy!

Can they find the final petal?

Roses Need Rescuing!

"Here we are, the Chaney Palace Flower Show," Mr. Walker said, looking at the steady stream of people heading toward the entrance. He smiled at his daughter, Rachel, and her best friend, Kirsty Tate. "What a flowery week we've had!"

"We love flowers!" Rachel said, giving Kirsty a secret smile.

"Especially since we met the Petal Fairies," Kirsty agreed in a whisper.

The girls linked arms as they followed their parents into the field where the flower show was taking place.

"What's in here?" Mr. Tate wondered aloud, as they approached a large tent. "Ah, the rose tent," he said, reading the sign on the entrance.

Kirsty and Rachel exchanged excited glances. Maybe the missing rose petal would be inside! A group of people were leaving the tent as the Tates and the Walkers approached.

"How disappointing," a man said gloomily. "I've never seen such unhealthy flowers!"

The Tates and the Walkers stepped inside the tent and Rachel saw that the

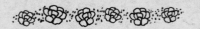

man was right. All the roses were drooping, their petals faded and withered.

"Let's go and see some of the gardens instead," Mr. Walker suggested, looking sadly at the drooping roses.

Rachel turned to Kirsty as they left. "The other flowers should be beautiful because we've already found the other petals and sent them back to Fairyland," she whispered.

Kirsty nodded. "But we've got to rescue these roses!"

There's magic in every book

The Rainbow Fairies
Books #1-7

The Weather Fairies
Books #1-7

The Jewel Fairies
Books #1-7

The Pet Fairies
Books #1-7

The Fun Day Fairies
Books #1-7

SCHOLASTIC

www.scholastic.com
www.rainbowmagiconline.com

HIT entertainment